WHAT THE SEAL SAW

Written by Sherry McMillan
Illustrated by Carla Maskall

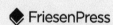

FriesenPress

One Printers Way
Altona, MB R0G 0B0
Canada

www.friesenpress.com

Copyright © 2021 by Sherry McMillan
First Edition — 2021

All rights reserved.

No part of this publication may be reproduced in any form, or by any means, electronic or mechanical, including photocopying, recording, or any information browsing, storage, or retrieval system, without permission in writing from FriesenPress.

ISBN
978-1-03-912004-4 (Hardcover)
978-1-03-912003-7 (Paperback)
978-1-03-912005-1 (eBook)

1. JUVENILE FICTION, ANIMALS

Distributed to the trade by The Ingram Book Company

Dedicated to

Alyson
Bo
Duke
Evan
Felix
Garret
Hayden
Haylee
Landen
Natalie
Rocco
Ronin
Violet

And those on their way.
May you always love stories as much as I love you.

Aunty Sherry

A shiny plump seal
All whiskers and eyes
POPS OUT OF THE WATER
What a surprise!

It looks around
WHAT DOES IT SEE?
I see the seal
And the seal sees me.

Then just like that

It disappears

WHERE DID IT GO?

It's under the pier.

Off it goes

SO SMOOTH AND SLICK

A seal is agile

A seal is quick.

THE SEAL SEES STARFISH

Bold and bright

On the legs of the pier

Clinging tight.

THEN DOWN, DOWN, DOWN

Through the dancing grass

It sees ten spiny legs

As a crab scuttles past.

Up out of the water

Then way down deep

All over the bay

ITS SECRETS TO KEEP.

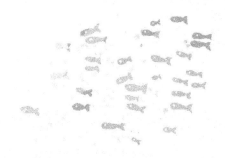

The seal sees a swizzle

Of silver-grey fish

DARTING AND DASHING

Wherever they wish.

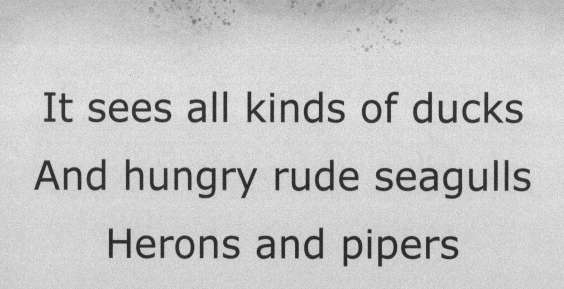

It sees all kinds of ducks

And hungry rude seagulls

Herons and pipers

STARLINGS AND EAGLES.

ALL HONKING AND FLAPPING

A noisy migration

The geese are a mystery

Of organization!

The seal swims out
To the ocean wide
IT KNOWS THE SHORTCUTS
It knows the tide.

It sees a giant

RAISE ITS WIDE GRACEFUL TAIL

Bubbles and barnacles

A glorious whale!

When stars come out
With a great gold moon
EVEN WAVES ARE HUSHED
With the call of a loon.

Sunrise and sunset

The seal watches the sky

A kaleidoscope of colour

DOES IT WISH IT COULD FLY?

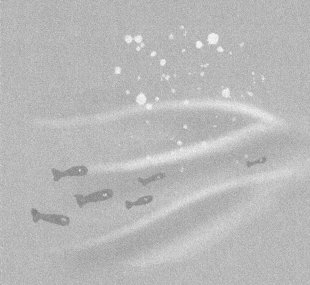

A seal has adventures

There's so much to see

It leads with its whiskers

AND CURIOSITY.

I love the ocean

I love the sea

I SEE THE SEAL

And the seal sees me!

Nurture a love of
nature and language
in little ones with
big imaginations.

Sherry McMillan is a resident of beautiful White Rock BC where she often takes her kayak into the bay. She finds herself talking to the seals when they pop up out of the water to visit. She asks them "What do you see?". From her conversations with seals, she wrote this book.

When she is not writing books or kayaking, Sherry feeds her curiosity by working in technology.

Carla Maskall is an award winning artist who has been drawing and painting since she was a child. She loves the ocean and can often be found either paddle boarding or plein air painting near the water.

Carla and Sherry have been friends since they were children.

Visit us at www.whatthesealsaw.com
#whatthesealsaw

Printed in the USA
CPSIA information can be obtained
at www.ICGtesting.com
LVHW061732010224
770636LV00014B/325

9 781039 120037